The Haves and Have Nots

A Fable on Inequality

The Haves and Have Nots

A Fable on Inequality

Arthur M. Mills, Jr.

Copyright © 2013 by Arthur M. Mills, Jr.

Published by Branching Plot Books

Editor: Tyler R. Tichelaar, Ph.D.

Cover design: Donna Casey

Library of Congress Control Number:		2013903936
ISBN:	Softcover	978-0-9860166-9-1
	eBook (Kindle)	978-0-9891840-0-7

DEDICATION

Christian and conservative values made this country great. Unfortunately, those values are under attack. Fortunately, there are still men and women in this country that are willing to stand up and fight for those values. One of those men is my uncle. Wayne Simmons has been the ideal God-fearing Christian and red-blooded American all his life. I dedicate this book to my Uncle Wayne – my hero – for teaching me Christian and conservative values. We need more men like him!

Arthur M. Mills, Jr. (Ray)

CHAPTER 1 – THE ARRIVAL

As predicted by Hummingbird, the flaming orb of the sun rose above the Douglas fir, the cedar, the oak, and the yew trees of Tolmie State Park at precisely seven-thirty that morning.

The chipmunks were blissfully preparing for a full day of food collection at a morning meeting somewhere closer to eight o'clock, when the picnickers' boats would row up to moor at their assigned buoys at the water's edge. Today's meeting would honor Mitch and his wife Tamias for being the maximum collection couple from just the day before.

Mitch and Tamias were experienced and knew just how short the summer lasted at Tolmie State Park, and how important it was to decide on the maneuvers involved in going for the nuts and seeds from picnickers, not to mention a separate foray for the acorn from the ground below the oak. Comfortably into middle age, Mitch and Tamias also had the necessary experience to refine their daily rounds of collection.

Now, the beautifully striped chipmunks were a group who were generous in their praise of their tribe. They worked hard and were insightful about who among them should be held up as the best example for the others; they knew recognition promoted industry and better collection for the beginning autumn days. Generally, the chipmunks were thought of as being an industrious lot, sometimes bringing about change, which Old Owl said led to biodiversity and the ecosystem, to planting seedlings and improving the environment. But the chipmunks preferred to go about their own business and leave such assessment to those who knew.

Today, however, just as their morning meeting was ending with its usual rounds of backslapping and jaw fur wiping, with a general sense of bonhomie and looking forward to what more the day could bring, they stopped short. Mitch prided himself on keeping a keen eye out for the best of nuts and seeds, and even the odd caterpillar and tiny egg, but he stopped short too, wondering what had caught everyone else's attention.

By now, the sun had risen to such an extent that it cast its light far and wide and was no longer the fiery orb of early morning. And then, Mitch saw. For the first time in his year-and-a-half-old life, he saw a normal-sized, mostly blue, bird with a black ring around its neck and a blue crest. Its chest and underbelly were soft white. It flew lazily in and perched on the ground near the astonished chipmunks, took a good look at them, and called out to its mate still in the air.

Mitch held his breath for a minute, and then the leader of the chipmunks offered a tentative "Hi."

He received back a very exuberant, "Hi, I'm Javlin." A general round of introductions followed and some more formal wing and hand shaking.

Soon, the next bird landed beside Javlin, and then another, and another. They jabbered and twitched a great deal, arguing about who was going to grab the fattest and juiciest snail. The chipmunks took a good step back and uttered a jittery "ugh!" in unison.

However, being of a polite nature, the chipmunks went on their way. And the blue birds went on their own as well. They had breakfast, and seemed to be having a mid-morning meeting of their own, using their own outside language. Mitch, however, thought that he had caught one cry, which sounded fairly close to the noises of the rusty pump just past the park entrance.

Mitch spoke to Tamias now as they charted out their collection strategy. "I will get seeds in the morning, nuts in the afternoon, and a careful stacking in the larder in our underground home in the evening." After that, he resolved to seek out Hummingbird (if he could get him to stop for a second) and Old Owl, who would only be up and about at dusk, to ask about their newest families in Tolmie State Park.

Tolmie State Park is on the edge of a spectacular estuary in the United States' far northwest, near Olympia, Washington. The park has only a quarter mile of beach but acres of forest. Free-spirited humans from nearby cities such as Olympia row in through the rivers and estuary, and scores of animals either live there or arrive when the weather, or the bountiful food Tolmie State Park has to offer, tempts them. Some birds come there to lay their eggs and wait for them to hatch, and in winter, chipmunks and some other animals go into their burrows there for weeks or more than a month, to wait for spring and have their babies.

So the arrival of the free-spirited blue birds led by Javlin wasn't too unusual, except that by noon, most of the insects and animals, and of course, the birds in Tolmie State Park had noticed them. The blue birds had arrived in a couple of batches since breakfast time. They twittered and sang, ate, argued, and played lazily. They weren't fast fliers, but seemed to deliberate everything they did. In fact, they seemed to be more interested in style than substance.

It would be late afternoon by the time Coyote noticed the newcomers. He was an old coyote, now given to waking up long after the sun had passed its zenith, and on this day, he had been dreaming of a nice juicy chipmunk. Coyote was also notorious for eating anything in Tolmie State Park (and elsewhere) and rued the fact that he had often stalked, but never managed to catch, a chipmunk.

Mitch and Tamias, on the other hand, had scurried about all day, collecting a couple of acorns the young oak had shed and whole nuts from where the humans had left them for little animals like themselves. Their cheek pouches bulged as they darted toward their burrow with its entrance formed by a gnarled arch-shaped tree root behind the fourth row of maples.

On many of their journeys in and out, they passed the batches of noisy blue crested birds. But the chipmunks had work to do, and Javlin and his tribe of birds had food to find, so each would take a look at the other (a friendly look, Mitch hoped) and carry on their way. Every time, Mitch told himself that he would have to find out who they were, though their presence toward the end of summer could only be welcomed.

And so it was nearly eventide before Mitch could venture off to find the answer to his question from that morning. He knew Hummingbird would be getting ready for his second round of nectar feeding, and that he might just catch him as he hovered here and there, among the woodland flowers. Mitch kept a sharp eye on the air around him. Hummingbird would be easily distinguishable from today's slow-flying blue birds, and Hummingbird would know. Owl would only be up later in the evening.

However, Coyote saw Mitch approaching him, scurrying in short darts from behind one maple to another, apparently at ease about predators at this time of day. He thought of the dream he'd had during that afternoon's siesta. Could he bring it to fruition? Could he really ensnare the most industrious of chipmunks? Coyote's nose and tail itched to align into a straight line, to point. But he told himself that he wasn't young, and that he must be patient, even cautious.

And so Coyote waited behind the first row of maples, sitting as still as he could. He told himself that he must hold his breath if he were to pounce when the time was right.

However, half a minute into his patience and breath-holding exercise, there came about a rusty sounding twittering, with the swish of slow-flying wings above Coyote's head.

Mitch heard the creaky noise too, and he knew that the new blue birds were agitated about something. And then, he saw Coyote waiting to pounce. Mitch was so alarmed that he dropped the little seed he was carrying in both paws as an offering for Hummingbird, and jumped high into the air. He landed on his feet in an instant, turned tail, and ran back in the direction from which he had come.

And so Mitch had escaped being Coyote's meal for the nth time. He made it to his burrow but paused only after he had reached the safe confines of the outer sleeping area—and Tamias. He told her about his quest, and his close shave—and how the objects of his curiosity had been the ones to warn him.

But now Tamias' curiosity was up, as well. She gave Mitch a warm hug and an acorn cup full of still warm dew to drink. She sang him a twittery song as he relaxed, and then she broached the subject again. "Mitch, we do have to find out."

The two waited a little longer for the shadows to lengthen, and then, they set out together. Tamias was familiar with the defensive darting that Mitch employed on such occasions. They would wait behind a tree, their bushy tails quivering but safely out of viewing range by any bird or animal attempting to sniff them out. And then, when they were sure that the coast was clear, they would make another long run. The two little chipmunks carried on like this until they reached the great hollow.

The great hollow was actually an ancient aspen tree, long since struck by lightning and without leaves. They could see Old Owl framed at the entrance to his hollow, his family preparing to go out for the night, to see what the forest might allow them by way of a wholesome meal. Old Owl seemed to know that he might be asked to share his store of information.

He greeted Mitch and Tamias with his customary hooting, and asked, "What can I do for you?"

So Mitch told him about the newcomers and asked, "Do you know what kind of birds they are?" After Mitch asked, Old Owl paused for so long that Mitch thought he might not have heard, or that he might have gone right back to sleep.

However, Old Owl had heard the question perfectly and was racking his mind for a perfect fit. Finally, he had it. When he did speak, it was to make sure. He asked again about the color of the birds' collar, the color of their crest, the nature of their chirruping, and their general nature.

Then, Old Owl went back to thinking. Finally, he told the eager chipmunks that the birds were blue jays—and that they mainly fed on nuts and seeds such as acorns and fruit. They also ate creepy-crawlies. He told them that blue jays typically glean food from trees, shrubs, and the ground, and sometimes, they hawk insects from the air. He also mentioned snails. Then, he said, "The bird's name comes from its noisy, garrulous nature, and sometimes, it's also called a jaybird."

Mitch knew that all this eagerly awaited information was correct. He already knew about the worms. He told himself that it didn't matter about the nuts and seeds and fruit or even the acorn. Tolmie State Park had enough for everyone. But somehow, Mitch no longer felt good.

CHAPTER 2 – THE ENCOUNTER

The next day dawned equally bright. The chipmunk meet took place at the usual time while Javlin and his blue jays went about their grooming, singing, and then breakfast. The chipmunk topic of discussion today was how to maintain high levels of productivity, despite environmental distractions. Some half-a-dozen chipmunks spoke enthusiastically. Mulch, who lived in the neighboring burrow to Mitch, said this topic would be better evaluated in qualitative terms because their productivity extended to creatures large and small in the park, and it didn't only benefit their group of chipmunks.

Mitch felt mighty proud of Mulch's perspicacity. Now, they could share this information with Hummingbird and Old Owl. However, midway through the animated meet, the chipmunks became aware of something they had never encountered before. They found that others in Tolmie State Park were paying heed to what they were speaking about. Javlin was paying close attention to the minutes of their meet.

The blue jays were hopping around on the ground near them as they had the day before. It was breakfast time for them, and they were also paying heed to their meal. One swooped up to carry off an unsuspecting spider, which had been tentatively sliding down its silvery thread from a branch in the tree above. Another sampled the pine nut from a low hanging branch. But as busy as they were, Javlin seemed to be making sure they remained close to the chipmunk meet. And as busy as their pecking and gobbling kept them, they seemed to listen carefully to the chipmunk proceedings.

"Was this what they meant by environmental distraction?" thought Tamias. "Or are they planning to get started on their own morning meets?" That would be extremely organized of them, she decided—on their second day in Tolmie State Park! She wondered why she had wondered about all this, and then she knew. From the manner of the blue jays' need for argumentative, sometimes fun (to them) activities, she knew that being frightfully organized wasn't something they could be.

Later that day, Tamias was able to confirm this notion.

She had had a long struggle with a pinkish brown worm, which had more of itself hidden in the earth than out—it was of a length she hadn't expected. When at last Tamias had won the battle, she decided the worm was worth carrying back to their larder to share with Mitch at suppertime, though it would obviously not keep till autumn. She would just have to proceed to drag it back home.

It would be a long haul, but hopefully, worth the effort when Mitch and she sat down for supper that night. Tamias embarked on her journey, remembering to keep her chin up and her cheek pouches out.

On the way, she encountered a trio of blue jays, in their usual twitchy, jabbering mood. One had strung a miniature mandolin with long grass and was actually trying to tweet a chirrupy tune. The other two, it seemed, were dancing a mini-minuet. Tamias remembered her curiosity from the evening before, the curiosity that had driven Mitch and her to listen to Old Owl's sage observations.

Now, she paused for an instant. The dragged tail of the worm flopped untidily around her. She hoped the musically inclined blue jays would understand her Tolmie State Park animal-language as she asked, "Hi. I'm preparing supper for my husband and myself. He's out, preparing to stock our larder for the autumn. What about you and your lot?"

The blue jays stopped, it seemed, in wonder. They turned around to gape at her burden and burst out laughing. "Preparing supper!...stocking food for later! This sure is rich of you! Why on earth do you want to work hard when there is so much on offer?"

The blue jays couldn't go back to their singing and dancing right away because they took up so much time laughing and poking fun at the notion of having to work to save for lean times. They said that no blue jay had ever had to work for a living. Whether it was a fat snail, or just-browned seeds or tourists' nuts, food would always be there for them. Life was for having fun and life would be short. "You don't have to spend your time shoring up for later, you know," they said to Tamias.

Now Tamias was a careful wife and had been a caring mother. Her babies had been tutored by her about storing and saving when they went out into the big world, and that was what they would be doing right now, since they had long left home. Tamias was a trifle offended at the blue jays' response to her simple question, and she felt exasperated by their behavior when there was so much to be done. But being of a polite nature, she covered up her disappointment and went on her way.

The strumming and twittering noises behind her resumed. A few paces off, she wondered about the rusty pump noises she could hear.

The fat worm was a good enough treat for Mitch and her to dine on, and she didn't bring up the blue jays as a topic for suppertime conversation. Tamias thought briefly about what the park would be like this year—would they have a winter fairyland, as they had the last year? Before she fell asleep, she also thought briefly about the birds. The geese, she knew, would soon fly south to greener pastures. But what about the blue jays? They wouldn't have food stocks like the hibernating bears—who didn't need any, anyway—or like their fellow chipmunks who would be up and about early tomorrow morning, again discussing the best way to go about things.

Mitch and Tamias slept well at night, their bellies full, and with the knowledge that even if they were middle-aged, they had the strength and energy to shore up for the colder months. And if the park was as pretty as it had been last year, they would still prefer to stay in their burrows—with maybe Mulch for company now and then.

All the chipmunks were going to be so very busy finding and storing food the next day—the best storage day in September, according to both Hummingbird and Old Owl—that they had decided to skip their early morning meet and get down to good, hard work. It would be like a starter's signal. They would have to practice hard now if they were going to save for the winter.

Mitch felt highly energized after the wholesome meal he'd had the day before, so he couldn't wait to get down to brass tacks. He darted out of their home at the crack of dawn, determined to be the first, the most industrious. He went down to the estuary's edge and was comforted by the boats that humans had stayed in overnight beside mooring buoys. It was a narrow strip of beach at Tolmie State Park, and Mitch was the only early morning wanderer along the shore.

A human boy in one of the boats saw Mitch and was entranced by the large chipmunk with stripes down its back. The boy, who was about thirteen, was with his father. They had brought their own high-energy provisions with them for their overnight trip, and the boy decided to toss some shelled peanuts to this early rising, most industrious chipmunk of all. Mitch, in turn, was overjoyed. He might be able to fill his own larder and Mulch's in one whole day!

But if he was going to enjoy the fruits of his labor to the fullest, he had some hard thinking to do. First, he buried all but one of the peanuts in the sand. That one he half-dragged and half-carried with him inland, toward the maples and his burrow. It would have to be a long drag because he was still nearly a quarter mile away.

Just inside the first row of woodland trees, he sensed a slow beating of wings just above his head. He had to strain to look up, what with his load, and saw a single blue jay making lazy eight swoops in the air and thoroughly enjoying itself. Mitch cast a friendly glance. Could it be Javlin, or could it be the same friend who had warned him about Coyote the other day? He wanted to tell that unknown friend how much he had appreciated the assistance.

But when he asked, the blue jay twittered back a "Don't know...don't care." The blue jay told Mitch that being a little blue jay was great fun, and the blue jays had wondered about the chipmunks on the ground, scurrying about, carrying things from here to there. Had someone given them work to do?

Mitch put his load down now. He put his hands on his waist as best he could, and he stretched his neck as far as he could. Mitch explained that all the woodland animals had to think about autumn...and then the winter. They couldn't eat all the summer foods right off, as delicious as they were, but had to judge which ones to put away. He recommended that the blue jays do the same because there wouldn't be a seed, any berry, or even a snail or an insect, when things got snowbound and cold.

Mitch now paused for a minute. The blue jay had carried on with its lazy eights. Had it heard? It turned out it had, because now it laughed again. In fact, its twittering rang out in mirth across the clear blue sky. "To have to save for times of hardship! What an absurd idea! Dear chipmunk, look at me! Look at all of us blue jays! Have you seen us carrying things around the way you chipmunks do? Yet this park is our oyster. We've come here to have a good time, and we intend to do so. It's not for us to have to worry about what may come later," he snorted.

For once, Mitch was at a loss for words. He had never encountered this sort of thing among all the insects, birds, and animals in his whole life. It was true that not everyone was as hard working as their band of chipmunks, but the others always paid heed to what they had to say on the matter, and some of them, like the geese, did have backup plans about what to do and where to go. But not to think about what would come after the summer! To think only of having a good time as long as their needs were plentiful! Mitch was aghast.

He switched the large peanut to his back because it might be easier to carry that way. He was right. His legs bent just a little, but he got back home in record time. Tamias wasn't there. She was out doing her own collecting. So Mitch scurried back to the beach for the next peanut, and thankfully, he met no more of the birds about on this trip.

The third time around, a couple of the blue jays did watch him from the branch of an elm, but when he looked up to say hello, he noticed that they were nudging each other, pointing at him with their wings and laughing at the sight of a chipmunk hauling a large peanut. So he ducked his head and went on his way.

Mitch held his peace till Tamias got home and they had groomed and cleaned themselves and laid out their supper. Then, unlike her, he did confide in her about his experience with the blue jays and their thoughtlessness, their take on not being bothered about the benefits of hard work. That was when Tamias told Mitch about the three mandolin strumming, singing, and dancing blue jays she had come across the other day, and her conversation with them.

That night, the two of them sat up and discussed matters late into the night. They wondered what lay in store for the blue jays, that year. But Mitch and Tamias didn't think of what could lie in store for themselves because they believed firmly in the benefits of hard work.

CHAPTER 3 – FINDERS KEEPERS

The next day, halfway through the chipmunk morning meet, Mulch came up to offer Mitch an acorn cup full of sunlit pine juice, a delicacy the chipmunks relished. That was when Mitch remembered the whole peanuts he had buried in the sand at the waterfront, some of it with Mulch in mind.

Mitch waited patiently for the meet to be over and participated as little as possible. The instant the meeting was done, he nodded at the blue jays, who had again gathered to listen to what the chipmunks were about, and then took off, racing to the water's edge. Mitch thought he recognized the boat. Today, the boy was helping his father with ropes. They seemed to be unraveling theirs from the buoy and were getting ready to leave the park. Mitch hoped they would be back sometime before the summer ended.

Mitch started scuttling about, looking for the peanut burial spots of the day before. He had taken the trouble to bury each separately and mark the spot with a tiny starfish. He should, really, have come back the day before, because some of the starfish may simply have swum off when the tide had come in.

At last, Mitch identified all the spots, and dug with his tiny front paws as quickly as he could. He could see that three of the peanuts were still there, but two weren't. "Never mind," he told himself. Given the distance back to his and Mulch's burrows, and the effort it had taken the day before to get a couple of whole peanuts back, all five would have taken days. Then he got busy getting the fattest of the peanuts home.

It was the same drill as the day before, and he chose the same route that would take the least time. Mitch had reached the woodland trees and looked out for his friend, the blue jay who had been engaged in looping loops the day before. He wasn't there today, but the other three, who had sat on a branch, were now on the ground. They were playing with—a large peanut shell.

The blue jays had obviously picked the inside clean and were happy at what they had got. When they saw Mitch, they asked whether they could relieve him of his heavy burden. They laughed, hopped close to him, and sang twitteringly.

Mitch asked where the blue jays had gone for their peanut. The three were only too happy to tell Mitch. They laughed as they said, "Why, we just had to go back to the beach, the direction you had come from yesterday, and we saw these carefully marked spots. We dug, and look at what we found!" They looked boldly back at Mitch.

Mitch was aghast. He was tongue-tied for a minute, but then he said (though he stuttered), "But birdies, what if some other animal had buried it for himself?" The blue jays shrugged and said in unison, "Too bad." That night, Mitch would have more to say to his wife.

At the next morning's chipmunk meet, one very young chipmunk floated the motion to discuss stores that were going missing. When a couple of the young chipmunks complained vociferously, Javlin, who was hovering on a low branch with a bunch of blue jays, lent an ear. Javlin and the blue jays were quiet, as they tended to be when the chipmunks discussed matters close to their hearts.

Later at the same meet, the more mature chipmunks counseled the young ones, telling them that they should give more thought to how and where they stored their winter foods. A good well-planned burrow, they were told, usually had a larder at the end, just before the dining space. All stores were best secured there.

Mitch kept his own counsel. After all, he hadn't made sure that all the peanuts had got safely into his larder, or Mulch's. He hadn't worked hard enough that one day when he had left a couple of nuts buried on the beach. It had simply been a case of "Finders keepers."

The next week turned out to be 'Wild Berry Week' at Tolmie State Park. Javlin and the blue jays were exuberant and they were everywhere, reaching for berries in every color with their beaks. The chipmunks industriously gathered the ones that hung from low branches or ripened and fell to the ground. The blue jays' happy song filled the skies around Tolmie State Park that week, and even Old Owl came out to clap his wings early in the evening.

Hummingbird also made an appearance. Wisely, Hummingbird had successfully sought his wife with aerial pyrotechnics that could outstrip the blue jay's lazy eights. He would dive close to her, his feathers making a loud whining sound near the bottom of an oval trajectory. That trajectory also covered the whole of his feeding territory. Hummingbird didn't need to go down to the water's edge the way Mitch did because Tolmie State Park wasn't only covered in different types of trees, but also in wildflowers, from which Hummingbird drew nectar, not to mention the insects that hovered around those flowers. Hummingbird hovered near open flowers and sipped from red flowering currant, salmonberry, and honeysuckle.

Hummingbird's wife would build her nest over last year's nest, closest to the ground in a conifer. But this summer, she had been joined by other hummingbird wives. And they chose to build among huckleberry bushes, alders, blackberries, or drooping conifer branches. They had built early in the breeding season. Then as the summer wore on, they were joined by still more hummingbirds who had to build high in deciduous trees where it was cooler.

Soon, there was a hummingbird hum noticeable among the blue jays' twittering songs and the chipmunk chatter. Old Owl only hooted after dark, preferably when he left his great aspen hollow. Hummingbirds began to mark their nests with soft moss, and line them with plant down, covering them on the outside with lichen and bark, the whole thing held together by spider webbing. As for the contents, each nest had two eggs for the hummingbird wives to sit on.

Of course, a great hum was heard over Tolmie State Park when the eggs hatched and the mothers hovered to and fro, sipping and feeding their little ones with nectar. This went on for weeks, till they were old enough to do their own hum, their own feeding, and their own nest building. Some of them simply hummed south.

Best of all, the hummingbirds were strongly attracted to red flowers, although they also frequented pink, orange, or other colored flowers. They also preferred flowers shaped like a tube or trumpet. They had long beaks and even longer tongues, which they used to good advantage to feed at flowers that were too long and thin for anything else—such as bumblebees, who were too fat, and tiny ants, who tended to get lost in them.

The hummingbirds would insert their beaks into a flower to drink the nectar, and at the same time, sticky pollen grains would cling to the sides of their beaks. When a hummingbird visited its next flower, some of the pollen grains would be transferred, and if both flowers were the same species, pollination would take place. In this way, hummingbirds fed from the profusion of colorful wild flowers in Tolmie State Park and elsewhere, and they carried on propagating the ecosystem.

The hummingbirds, therefore, were as welcome as everyone else to the park. They used their welcome to their best advantage too, zipping from what was one ideal flower for them to the next. They weren't only feeding on the nectar; they were pollinating the flowers, which in turn allowed the plant to produce fruits or seeds. They brought small specks of color to the colorful profusion of flowers which they frequented, as well.

The blue jays had been welcomed partly for this reason too. They brought specks of darting blue to Tolmie State Park. Not only that, but they brought an entirely new range of song to the park, quite complemented by the hummingbirds' hum. In any case, they added to the natural diversity of a rich park, diverse in plant and animal life, and especially in the many birds who flocked there. The blue jays, like the hummingbirds, had arrived as soon as spring announced itself.

However, unlike the neat, many-layered hummingbird nests, the blue jays lay their nests in trees near which they wouldn't let their other bird friends or small animal neighbors come. In fact, the blue jays took to a new kind of sport now. If any bird or small animal came near, even unmindfully, they would let them come a little close; then a chattering flock would descend on the innocent creature, threatening to peck at it.

Soon, the blue jays' trees stood out apart from the others in the forest. The word was out that the blue jays' trees would have to be left alone, and that no one should go near their nests.

Then, there was Big Ant, some of whose tribe was always eaten by the hummingbirds. If Mitch had one hummingbird friend, he had many ant friends. They, too, were as socialized as the chipmunks, but mostly within their own sort. Mitch, having lived longer than most, was their friend on the "outside." Also, they knew a great deal.

They knew, for instance, that they had to be any place where there were plants and flowers, and they had done so for millions of years. They formed colonies which also took up territories here and there in Tolmie State Park. They had their work divided, and they weren't in the least like chipmunks, all of whom did the same sort of work through the year. Nor were they like the blue jays, who sang and danced and ate what was on hand.

They were similar to the hummingbirds, perhaps, in their need for caloric nectar, but the workers among the ants were known to collect for everyone in their colony, not just for themselves and their own babies. Old Owl declared that many tree species have seeds that are dispersed by the ants. That was because the ants took the trouble to transport the seeds to safety below the ground.

All in all, the animals at Tolmie State Park agreed that the tiniest among them, the ants, performed many ecological roles that were beneficial. Old Owl stepped in again, saying that the manner in which they dug tunnels for their colonies helped to aerate the soil, too. Old Owl had said this to Mitch, who had scampered off to tell his friend ants the very next day. He couldn't quite see their expressions, but his friend Big Ant said they were mighty satisfied at what they heard.

However, during an early morning chipmunk meet on the ecological balance at Tolmie State Park, when Mitch expounded on all that he had picked up, the blue jays, who had been listening carefully, seemed to burst into chirrupy laughter. Tamias was a trifle offended at the manner in which the blue jays seemed to discount what her husband had to say, and she shook her head at Javlin, but she only got a wink and more chirrupy laughter back.

But all in all, and unknown to most, the plants and animals at Tolmie State Park were doing well that year and especially by the time autumn came around. They all had food to fill their stomachs, and the choicest of foods at that. All the groups who could had had their babies and were busy teaching them the ways of life and the ways of the world.

Everyone was busy, even if one new entrant, a winged group of blue jays brought in by Javlin, sometimes poached on what some of the others were working hard to store for the winter months when food would be scarce and the earth was known to yield less. But that was the nature of their ecological cycle, till the next spring and the next summer, when, hopefully, matters would be back where they started.

But would this paradise last for long?

CHAPTER 4 – THE INEQUALITY

One night in October, Old Owl hooted and Owless screeched a great deal. Mitch and Tamias, safe in their burrows, heard. Could the birds be signaling a danger outside at night? Though his innate senses had kept him alert and awake, Mitch decided that whatever it was could be investigated in the morning.

But then, he heard a scratching and his tiny chipmunk hairs stood on edge. It was a bright moonlit night, so someone was about doing his own investigating. And Old Owl was warning them—to stay at home.

The next morning, Mitch found the signs of who had come by, and for what. But to ask Old Owl about it meant a longish wait till dusk. Then Old Owl told Mitch that Coyote and his pack had come back from the great city. They said that they had quite liked what they had seen in Olympia and especially the delicious scraps of food that people tended to discard, far easier to snack on than the difficult-to-catch chipmunks, but still, they—and their leader—had felt a little homesick for good old Tolmie State Park.

As was the coyotes' tendency, and not being as well-socialized among the six of them as the chipmunks, or even the hummingbirds, blue jays, or ants, they had disagreed on a number of matters on the way back. They had agreed on one thing, though—that they would look around at nighttime.

By the time the coyotes arrived, the moon was up and they thought that come morning, they would need to find homes for themselves, like everyone else. Coyote went looking for his old burrow but it had simply collapsed. Another coyote decided to scratch one for herself, and chose a spot near the gnarled root in the fourth row of maples—Mitch's home! Well, she scratched and scratched, but the tough root had other ideas about other burrows and probably dissuaded her.

Old Owl had witnessed all this, and had called out in true distress, knowing that some innocents should be warned. All in all, the coyotes, or the senior most among them, had settled for an old disused wooden water barrel and had, at the same time, managed to announce their re-arrival. Given their grayish-beige color with patches of brown on the face and front legs, they intended to stay through the winter. Nobody in Tolmie State Park cared to think of what they would have to eat without the delicious cooked scraps in Olympia. The chipmunks hoped they wouldn't have to forage for their food off living morsels.

One day on a joint foray, Mitch and Mulch came across a gorgeous beehive bursting with honey. Big Bear had been lured to it by the delicious aroma, and he had even managed to take a swipe at the hive before the angry bees had chased him off. Now, the hive was lying on the ground and the bees were wondering whether they would have to conduct their business at that level.

Mitch and Mulch nibbled away a chunk where the honey flowed while they discussed matters, and they decided it was worth trying to carry it back. It would be a long haul, but hopefully, worth the effort. Mitch and Mulch, who had been jointly hauling a fragment of a delicious sweet-smelling hive, stopped in wonder as they passed the water barrel, which now lay on its side. It no longer housed an old coyote. It had five coyote pups looking out in wonder at the world of Tolmie State Park near the barrel mouth!

Mitch and Mulch couldn't help doing what they did next. They dragged their hive fragment over to give it to the cute little pups. One even came forward to play, but a dark fur shape pounced out from inside. It was their mother. Her nose was wrinkled and she had a little snarl. "Now, if we could get a couple of tiny baby chipmunks instead..." she was saying. Mitch and Mulch jumped a couple of feet backwards.

Mulch was all for a quick getaway, but Mitch thought it might be worth staying, and spreading the chipmunk credo. His voice may have quavered a bit, but it might be a good time to introduce the pups to Tolmie Animal-Language and to good habits. "It's going to be winter soon, you know, Mother Coyote," he said. "It's a good time to search a bit in the coyote trails and bring in nutritious foods for your little ones. Why, you may even find things that will keep for the winter. Your pups need to be fed then, as well."

He thought the mother was actually giving his oration some thought. But then she looked up quizzically as a chirrupy voice chipped in, "Look around for food? That's ridiculous! Make the best of what you have here and now, is what I, will have you know!" This remark was followed by the twittery blue jay laughter of many blue jays—laughter that the chipmunks had by now come to know so well.

Mother Coyote now looked decidedly angry. She shooed her pups back in the barrel and swished her tail at the blue jays. They went off in a flurry of wings, their near-mock laughter fading away toward the top of the nearest tree. Mitch was flabbergasted at the interruption, but he hoped those little pups would have food to eat when it was cold and Tolmie State Park less hospitable with its largesse.

He also wondered what the blue jays were going to do because he could see no signs of their taking his or Tamias' or Mulch's or any of the chipmunks' advice to heart. In fact, any talk of the benefits of work or about saving tended to be met with derision by them. Hummingbird worked on its calories and Old Owl was out and about every night, for it was meaty morsels that he looked for. But the blue jays simply ate what they happened upon without thought for the future.

In November, the forest almost appeared to be on fire when looking at it from high up in the sky. The trees' leaves had turned to gold, then pinkish gold, then reds and brownish maroons. Everyone still in Tolmie State Park was bustling about, and a great many animals, large and small, would call out to one another as did the birds who were still there.

The animals carried on working hard while the hummingbirds prepared to depart for sunnier climes. "There are, still lands where the bright flowers grow," they said to their friends. Their chicks now had grown into young hummingbirds, who would be strong enough for the long distances their flocks intended to fly.

The chipmunks sang come December. There was, too, a very satisfactory nip in the air, and the thought of the longer nights in the comfort of his or her own burrow with a well-stocked larder was now on every chipmunk's mind.

Old Owl, of course, was snug in his worn hollow. Some of the coyotes had finally managed to dig a great burrow, and the quickly-growing pups were quite thrilled at the idea of moving house.

The chipmunks now covered large tracts of ground, fetching and carrying. Old Owl had the night times to himself, as always. The blue jays remained in a frenzy of activity, chirruping and observing, dancing and singing, admiring themselves, and pecking at food. But those glorious colored trees were winding up too, giving forth a few berries, mostly dried, but no plump fruit. What on earth were the blue jays pecking at? For even the snails were retreating into crannies and crevices in rock and bark in the safety of their shells, leaving very few telltale silvery trails now.

This time, it was up to the curiously concerned chipmunks to hover and dart not-so-far from the blue jays to find out. But the ones who did drew a sharp breath of still more concern. The birds were gobbling at extremely choice nuts—nuts that only the chipmunks knew where to go for, and where to get them to—a chipmunk larder. The blue jays seemed to have a profusion of pine nut, acorn and

28

beech nut, chestnut and hazelnut. But they hadn't been seen to collect them. Where on earth had they come from?

When they asked, the chipmunks got a cheeky "Finders keepers" in reply. Now, what could have brought that on? Javlin quivered his tail feathers in impatience. He would have to say something. But what he said was even more mystifying. "It isn't fair that some small animals—maybe the same size as us, have everything—not to mention everything put away for when, as you have often reminded us, the times when Tolmie State Park is bound to be less hospitable. Well, if we can't labor for the foods you do, we simply acquire them."

Acquire them? But how?

This time, it was Old Owl who ruffled his wings and looked fiercely gruff at the chipmunks, his eyes piercing through his perfect circles beneath his brows. "I found out the hard way. I took a look at the bottom of my hollow, where Owless would store nuts. I suggest that all of you go take an inventory of your larders."

It was turning colder day-by-day, and winter was nearly upon them. The little chipmunks hoped Old Owl was wrong, but they did as they had been told. They went to check.

It was heartbreaking, especially for the younger couples. Their stocks had been broken into. They had all lost provisions that they had all labored hard to put by for themselves, some for their children.

Tamias wept when she discovered their hard-earned loss. Mitch tried, ineffectually, to comfort her with his arms around her sobbing head, patting her back. The chipmunks had to call an emergency late morning meet. Strangely, the blue jays didn't linger this time to listen. They seemed instinctively to know what it was about.

The chipmunk morning meet was no longer early because, as more and more of them went into semi-hibernation, they no longer woke very early at sunrise. Mitch and Tamias had been through two winters and were often called upon at the late morning meets for advice on how best to tackle the cold months, and how not to take up too much energy looking for food. "If you have followed our work habits and storage ethics for the many months since the summer, you could eat from your own stores," the older chipmunks would often advise.

Bear had gone to sleep for the winter in his rock enclosure, and the flowers had wound up flowering. Hummingbird had advised his brethren to fly south anyway, to lands where color still remained. But the coyotes had sworn to stay on, going back to Olympia and other cities only when it would turn warm.

During Tamias' long drawn-out siesta one afternoon, she was awoken by a scratching on the outside ground, which must have been near her burrow.

She remembered how a coyote had come around one night a month or two ago. "Not again!" she thought. She would have to tackle the intruder. Tamias got up and poked a cautious nose out of her front door, making sure of the daylight. She couldn't see any coyote or any of the pack, which would have had to stray far from its trail in any case. And then she heard a rustling of feathers but no chirping. Finally, she craned her neck to see Javlin straining his neck from a low branch to look at her. Two other young blue jays were with him, looking at Tamias and her burrow entrance expectantly. One of them still carried a grass mandolin, now a little beaten up.

In a trice, the three of them had hopped down on the ground in front of her. Tamias wished that it had been one of the coyotes because she was always unsure how to handle Javlin and his lot of aggressive blue jays. She was also thinking of all the missing chipmunk stores. But Javlin and the young blue jays only seemed to want to talk, and Tamias told herself that she would have to calm her suspicions.

Rather than speak to Tamias, however, Javlin was now talking to the young ones. He said, "So you see, there are some small birds who don't get the best of what Tolmie State Park can give, and there are some small animals who do." Then he advanced toward Tamias, who naturally shrank back, unwittingly exposing the entrance. Javlin was carrying on, "Come with me, and I will show you what I mean."

The trio managed to squash in through the burrow's entrance. The two young ones were looking expectant. Javlin now made a scary face at Tamias and demanded to know where the nuts were. When his intentions finally dawned on her, she refused to budge. How dare he try and help himself from the chipmunks' hard-wrought food stores? But Javlin had no intentions of backing down. He was intent on teaching his lot how to go about what his kind did best: "acquiring."

Pushing Tamias aside, Javlin began to dart down the tunnel of Mitch and Tamias' home that led to the first storage area. He was winding his way beak first, as were the other two. The first larder held the most recently collected insects, and the three blue jays made short work of the store in very little time. They decided to go further in.

But this would be Mitch's peanut stores! This time, however, the three blue jays decided their stomachs were full so they picked up a nut each to carry away. Getting really greedy, they decided to go further in, to see what more they could come back for.

Now, Mitch's burrow was one of the most complex and best. It housed the couple's sleeping quarters, and had a now-empty nursery from the time their babies had lived here. All the larger spaces were connected by tunnels that Mitch had personally dug. In fact, some of the underground tunnels connected. They were also narrow, too narrow, Javlin soon found out; he would be unable to move his wings if he got lost underground.

As before, Javlin led the way, darting out with his fellow errant-doers, the peanuts still clutched in their wings. They were irritable, and Tamias dared not stand in their way. But she wondered, as she had before, where all this was going. She was going to find out soon enough. Right now, she just worried about their meals and snacks when the snow came. When Mitch came back that evening, her voice broke as she told him in detail about the raid she had suffered that day, and the mystifying conversation she had heard.

Mitch was all for rounding up his pals and getting support from the other animal friends to prevent future invasions of his or any other chipmunks' burrow by the blue jays. He set about the task and organized a meeting, but in the end, Javlin and his tribe took over. Javlin fluttered to and fro in the cold and asked for a birds-of-a-feather and animals-of-fur conclave. Surprisingly, most came, barring the ones who had already gone into hibernation.

When the conclave began, the chipmunks were sure of their ground. They started to speak up in their squeaky high voices, but they were quickly shushed into silence by Javlin. He held forth now, saying that he had been forced to hear chipmunk speech on many a morning. "It is now time for me to speak. As a blue jay, I, Javlin, would like to put forth a couple of points that affect us blue jays and all of the rest of you." The others wanted to hear more, but in the back of their minds, there may have been growing a tiny speck of fear.

It was true, the chipmunks knew, that they had often discussed matters among themselves, but most of the time, while the chipmunks had talked, the rest of the birds and animals had listened and agreed. Now, the blue jay wished to be heard. It was only natural and would be polite on the chipmunks' part to let Javlin go ahead. Once he began, however, the chipmunks wondered how they would get a word in.

Javlin had taken up position on a low outreach of the park's spreading Arbutus tree, with its sweet-tasting lumpy red berries from the season before, which appeared at the same time as the tiny white flowers. Some of the blue jay teens quickly fashioned an Arbutus leaf megaphone for him. When he held it importantly to his tiny beak, his voice was much magnified. He looked determined, and everyone wondered what it was that he wanted so desperately to say.

"Brothers and sisters of Tolmie State Park," Javlin began. "I have called you here today to talk to you directly, about those who steal our food from our mouths…from our children's mouths. They call it storing. I call it hoarding. *They* are the real thieves." Javlin paused for effect while pointing directly at the group of surprised chipmunks. The air seemed even more frozen on the ground now. Steal? Hoard? This couldn't be!

CHAPTER 5 – THE ASSEMBLY

It seemed to be the blue jays' big announcement day, and Javlin was holding forth. But a high-pitched, squeaky, inflamed chipmunk voice was begging to be heard, from the sidelines. Some of the chipmunks pushed Tamias forward. She stood on a bough below Javlin. She didn't have the advantage of the Arbutus leaf megaphone, but she spoke loudly enough that everyone could hear her.

Tamias was obviously emotionally overcome. But she managed to get her words out all right. "It isn't saving by or for unjust means, you know, friends. We save so we have something to fall back on when the season is lean, as it is now, and will be more so later." And then, she related her experience when Javlin and the two young blue jays had raided her home, the burrow she shared with her husband.

Tamias didn't have a megaphone, but her voice seemed to penetrate. "We don't steal, I can tell you. We chipmunks work hard and save. We warned our friends the blue jays of what was to come. If they don't have enough now that winter is here, the blue jays are getting what they deserve. They are society's free-loaders!" A rustling paw clapping came from the chipmunks when she had finished. They agreed totally with her.

But the blue jays didn't agree. Javlin's brows were knitted when he got his breath back; he looked apoplectic with rage. He tapped the outside of his homemade leaf megaphone and began to thunder, "It's the chipmunks who are greedy, mean, and prejudiced against other animals." Again, he paused and lowered his hand-held device, moving his head and his eyes to take note of the effect he was having on the assembled souls.

There was a stunned silence. Could they be hearing what they were hearing? Through the silence came cries of blue jays whooping in their native tongue. They were cheering their leader's words. Javlin was satisfied at the effect of his speech. He took a deep breath and prepared to carry on. Plenty of other types of birds were still left at Tolmie State Park. A little rabble-rousing would do no harm. "Yes, they are prejudiced against non-chipmunks—all other animals, in fact. And I would say they are especially prejudiced against flying animals. The ones who do better than them. It's the chipmunks who have caused such disparity in *our* land. Our land has so much to offer, but *they* allow other animals to suffer when times are lean."

Another long silence followed while all this began to sink in. Other flying animals? All the birdies puffed out their chests. Old Owl had awoken with the great chirruping, and he had heard the tail end of Javlin's charge. He cocked his head to one side and wondered whether he should measure the merit of what had just been said. Maybe he should. Maybe, he could think of one or two occasions which could be held up as examples.

Now Owless remembered the excessive interest Mitch and Tamias had shown in the blue jays the evening they had arrived. Now, after what Javlin had said, she wondered what the real reason had been for their curiosity. Was it that they had taken a special measure of the types of birds? Owless was very concerned. Maybe for a change, she thought, she should side with someone of her own species, someone who could bring about some hope and change to Tolmie State Park; perhaps they had all been too skewed toward the chipmunks' apparent good sense to notice what they were really about.

Coyote Mother was at the animal meet. She had taken everything in. The coyotes might follow their age-worn trails about the park, but they, too, had craved city lights, resulting in the time they had gone to live on the outskirts of Olympia for some months. She knew that some hope and change brought thrills and excitement, even new cuisines such as scraps of cooked food, although the scraps were sometimes stale. Good sense was a good thing, but why should the animals of Tolmie State Park not want hope and change? "Those pesky chipmunks have been the center of attention for way too long," Mother Coyote thought to herself.

Now, she pondered what that change could be. For one, it could be a fresh new way of looking at problems…such as the ones Javlin was carrying on about. Well, he had an opinion about chipmunks that he was expounding now. It might not be a bad thing to pick up on it, if it could, at some time, ensure her a juicy chipmunk…that morsel that had been outside the reach of coyote diets up until now.

Coyote Mother, too, was now on the side of the blue jays. She was on the side of their rhetorical leader, Javlin.

Tamias knew that the tide had turned and that the crowd didn't favor her kind anymore. Horrifyingly, the other types of birds left in Tolmie State Park seemed to be handing over to Javlin some kind of support—support that seemed to inspire Javlin to a display of single wing power, however medium-sized he might be.

Javlin was waving his Arbutus leaf megaphone about, a bit like an army general at the head of his troops. He was circling his right wing about, paddling it above his head and goading everyone to the fore. The chipmunks were visibly shrinking back from their position out in front. But there was no stopping the marauders now. They rushed about, to and fro, barging in—entering any and all burrows at will. All the while, Javlin called out, "Look at those chipmunks, getting rich off the back of the *real* hard-workers, underprivileged classes." Most of the other animals joined in with the blue jays and praised the smooth-talking Javlin. Some of the animals became so entranced with Javlin's message that they began to faint in excitement.

Not to let a good crisis go to waste, Javlin continued, "From this day forward, I'll ensure such injustices as the one the chipmunks brought here will never occur under, on, or above the soil of Tolmie State Park." With the exception of the chipmunks, animals of all kind, birds of a feather as well as animals of fur, were under Javlin's spell.

Mother Coyote jumped to, snarling everyone away from her burrow and her now grown puppies. Javlin carried on with his rhetoric through all this, telling the other cross-looking blue jays that it was up to them to seek out and exhibit what some animals could hoard. They entered all the chipmunk burrows, which they appeared to have staked out in advance. They raided every one of them, leaving with their wings laden with spoils.

But they were carrying away carefully stored nuts and dried insects, even insect eggs and winter berries. The blue jays even descended on some small left-behind hummingbird nests and said they had found carefully hidden food hoards in these. They held all the spoils of their looting aloft, saying that they wished to demonstrate the disparity between the haves and have nots.

Owless could plainly see that the few dead mice at the bottom of her hollow would never compare with the glittering prizes of the raid so plainly held up for all to witness. She didn't have any bright red holly berries such as those that now emerged from the chipmunk burrows. The nighttime frost had rendered the remaining holly berries inedible for all animals, and Owless looked forward to a few of those edible berries that the chipmunks hoarded.

What about the others in the park? Wriggly Milk Snake had also popped out of his underground snake pit, camouflaged by frosty ground this December, to see what the huge ruckus was about. He reminded himself that he was a reptile, a shiny snake covered in white-black-red bands and of the sort that the others had been known to fear. Why was it that his scales now stood on end?

He seemed to have heard something about birds having evolved from reptiles. So did this lot of blue jays, who seemed to be on an extended raid, think that they had also progressed in making scary faces, running riot, and occupying the whole park? Apparently they did. The very next instant, a horrific thought struck him. Milk Snake didn't have a moment to lose as he popped back into his cranny to warn Mrs. Milk Snake to guard the snake eggs with her life.

Milk Snake had also been told about his striking resemblance to coral snakes and how this mimicry could scare potential predators. Did the blue jays know? He heard them call out. But it would only be the practical-minded chipmunks who knew the mnemonic to distinguish properly between the deadly coral snake and the harmless milk snake:

"Red on yellow will kill a fellow, but red on black is a friend of Jack."

Milk Snake wished he weren't so non-venomous. Now he was pushed into a decision by a small, sharp beak advancing threateningly toward him, and inside his snake hole. The pecking had already started, so he knew he might have to raise his hooded white flag to signal a truce. His wife and children from the last batch of eggs were doing this behind him just now. They weren't that keen to have their snakeskin split by the blue jays' sharp little beaks.

The blue jays were targeting not only the snakes—in their now frightfully aggressive charge, they had also got going on their normal diet. The snakes could see the effect of the beaks on snails, even the snails with shells—not counting the slugs, that is. The snakes wished they could wriggle back tail first. The birds were darting around in formation—and in cohesion, sometimes too quick, even for a zigzagging snake.

And what of the group that had supposedly brought about this loss of all sense on the part of the blue jays—the striped chipmunks of Tolmie State Park, the group that had long prided itself on its store of sound common sense? Could they stand steadfast in the mayhem wrought by the blue jays on this day?

The chipmunks, as reported, had at first retreated. They had remembered to stay together, as they tended to, being well-socialized animals. When they had been forced to witness the raids on their carefully laid burrows, they had shed many a tear, but they wouldn't speak out of turn, or behave differently from their normal manner. Now they had also witnessed that the blue jays' raids could go on for as long as the nasty little birds wished because they had cowed down any possible opposition. In fact, they seemed to have garnered support from previously ungarnered foes.

Was it a case of the sword rushing through a win? A case of the biggest bully getting a chance? Unhappily, so it would seem.

The chipmunks watched and waited for the mayhem to end, as they knew it would, ultimately. As for a reversal back to everyone's former manners, points of view, and general opinions—they weren't sure whether that would ever happen. The only thing the chipmunks—Mitch and Tamias, Mulch and his wife, and the many dozens more—were sure of was that they wouldn't have to behave in any manner dictated for them by the seemingly progressive-minded blue jays, the messiahs of everything-for-all.

After all, the chipmunks had developed their philosophy of what to do when times were lean, not to mention helping one another when they could, out of years of problem solving, and of sound logic that only what was correct was acceptable. So now, they cast aside loss of material goods, of all they were losing in the form of hard-accumulated foods. They stood firm in their conviction that they would agree on the wisdom of hard work—if not among anyone else, then among themselves.

The chipmunks said that all that was at stake now were the lack of work habits and ethics of a greedy few.

They didn't utter this in a manner that decreed that they would act superior to who may oppose them. They simply said it quietly among themselves, and to their neighbors who didn't mind listening to what they had to say. The chipmunks said it in many ways, and the information spread out. Everyone else came to hear that the chipmunks had decided to stand firm against the blue jays' lack of good practice habits, their lack of ethics.

Unfortunately, the chipmunks hadn't bargained for one thing. They were sure of their own convictions, but they mistakenly thought that the other groups of birds and animals—even snakes and other reptiles at Tolmie State Park—would somehow go back to thinking the way they had before the blue jays had turned everything on its head. The chipmunks were going to be wrong in this bit of logical thought.

The chipmunks would be the only ones who would see the merit of all they had decreed. The others would be either cowed, or bullied, or plain fearful. They wouldn't come back to being the way they were. Tolmie State Park wouldn't come back to being the haven it had been for all those who sheltered there.

The snow was falling thick and fast now. In nearby cities, human children were shoveling snow for a few bucks to clear the driveways. Christmas was signaled by a snow mantle that decorated the fir trees, leaving the red holly berry the only color on a holly decked bough. Christmas was followed by the New Year, when a few brave souls from Olympia ventured down to view the white wonderland of Tolmie State Park. The chipmunks and everyone, for that matter, stayed as far underground in their burrows as much as they could during this time.

The thing was, the chipmunks only semi-hibernated, and the blue jays had emptied their larders. The chipmunks no longer had their food stores. They were hungry, and most of them were starving. It wasn't only Mitch and Tamias. It wasn't only Mulch and his wife, but most of them, who had lost what they had worked so hard last autumn to store.

They came back up, hoping to discover a few forgotten rich pickings. It wasn't for them to raid others' burrows. Nor would they beg off the tall trees now asleep in the snow. Alas, there was nothing to be found, no matter how hard they looked, no matter how hard they hoped. The blue jays, high up in the boughs near the top of the cedar and the yew, the pine and the spreading oak, watched and mocked them as they ran here and there in their panic-stricken search, their stomachs rumbling, their memories conjuring images of what they had lost.

Needless to say, the blue jays, in their unreasonable rush, had either spilled or left the spoils of their loot to rot. They had gorged that day, but they had put nothing away. They had been rich for one afternoon—one evening. They were starving now as well. All the same, as was their nature, they kept a close watch on the futile comings and goings of the once-resourceful chipmunks, just in case.

But Tolmie State Park's larder was now bare. There was nothing to be found. Everyone would have to starve. Everyone would have to stay hungry. Though they were in a park that had been safe once upon a time, the blue jays' actions now had turned against everyone.

The chipmunks, for sure, were alone. There was no hope for them. Sadly, one by one, they gave up their spirits. Most of them died.

As for Mitch, when the end came, he said that he didn't mind. He had lived a good life up until now, and the chipmunk downfall couldn't be foreseen. There wasn't any way that any of them could have prepared for this calamity. Unfortunately for the little souls, there were no wakes and there were no funerals. But their friends, or the friends they had known during the last summer and autumn, did mark their passing.

CHAPTER 6 – THE BEGINNING OF THE END

However, the newest, the largest group who had migrated to Tolmie State Park the year before, the blue jays, decided that the death and subsequent near disappearance of the chipmunk population was a victory. They decided it was a victory that their group should celebrate, even rejoice over. Javlin chose the same Arbutus tree from which he had led the battle charge to declare his jubilation.

This time too, all of the animals in Tolmie State Park were present for the victory speech. It included those who had missed out the last time when Javlin had picked up the threads of argument and aggression. This gathering took place despite the ground being about a foot deep in snow, making it difficult for creatures such as Milk Snake and Ant to pop their heads up high enough as they now were forced to do, so they could see and hear their dear leader, Javlin.

Milk Snake had never slipped in his slither. Old Owl had never been so rudely awoken from his morning sleep. But it wasn't only them. Everyone present was really forced to be there. They were scared now, and they were scared for a different reason. Had they not come, they would have been worried about Javlin and his gang of blue jays, which now called themselves, "The Blue Youth."

Most of those gathered didn't really want to join in the victory celebration. Old Owl and Owless were secretly in mourning for their friends, but they felt they should hide their true feelings. What if the blue jays realized that they had earlier backed them up only because they had also hoped to get something for themselves? Everyone was going through similar, complex soul searching, and not all of it revealed the best of themselves to anyone.

Javlin proclaimed in a loud and boisterous voice, "The demise of the chipmunks' unjust and racist 'leadership' is a victory for all living things in Tolmie State Park. We are a free society now. A society where all are equal and all must contribute their fair share and will receive their fair share."

The animals and insects listened, but their spirit, naturally, wasn't there. Javlin and the blue jays had made sure that all would starve, especially the security-minded group who had put away for days and nights as cold as these. The blue jays had in a way forced them to leave the security of their snug burrows to go look for something to eat when they weren't scheduled to.

The blue jays had forced the chipmunks—and everyone else— out into the open, and the cold environment where no one could hunt or gather had killed their most industrious, most loved group of animals. Nor could they dwell on it; nor were they going to be allowed to put up a prayer since the blue jays believed prayer was a waste of time.

All life in Tolmie State Park was, indeed, miserable. It included not only the once-active animals and other bird groups, but the trees, plants, shrubs, and all vegetation as well. They couldn't speak of what they wished, and they couldn't admit to themselves what they wanted. Tolmie State Park was to become a very sad park, indeed.

The first to react was the forest and woodland cover. It simply seemed to sag. The tops of the trees began to reach downwards. The tree trunks and boughs followed suit. That meant that when the hummingbirds would come back in the spring and summer, the lower boughs would no longer be the vantage points to bag among the young hummingbird mothers. Nor did anyone want the topmost branches (which in any case were no longer the topmost) for the cooler air when it grew warm.

That summer, some of the trees began to register their opposition to the group that had seemingly won the tussle for survival. They simply refused to have any more to do with the blue jays—they didn't wish to house the blue jays in their boughs, provide shade for their jabbering meets, or want them skittering around through their leaves.

The great elms first turned bone dry, then withered, then they simply perished. The great oaks followed suit to become hollow, and the owls in this part of the world were at first pleasantly taken up with the sudden surge in available homes, but the putrefied mess at the bottom of the many available hollows became too much to stomach, not only for the resident and neighboring owls, but the mice and rats as well.

It was the same story with the yew and the alder, the once great arbutus tree that had started life in Tolmie State Park as a colorful rambling bush much loved by the littlest of birds and insects.

Strangely enough, the ruling blue jays, who had turned their initial victory into a jubilation over the demise of the chipmunks, carried on in the same vein at the death of the other forest life. Every time a species of tree, plant, or bush perished, the blue jays would fill the skies over Tolmie State Park with their sharp chattery cries, declaring that they had won because something had been vanquished. But, thought the other animals—though they could still not say so out loud—that something had been a life! As before, they kept quiet on the matter. And then, something, or someone else would slowly give in to the blue jays' all-consuming ways. It would receive no support from the rest, till it would grow exhausted and ultimately, perish.

Housing, however, for the animals appeared to be getting better and better. Milk Snake took up residence with his entire family in what had been Mitch and Tamias' burrow. Big Ant moved into Mulch's old burrow and then proceeded to extend the underground tunnels with the help of his ant armies. But in all wisdom, he kept them away from the blue jays. He hoped that if he ignored their mayhem, they might eventually give up or even go away. Big Ant waited and hoped because it now had turned to spring and some of the migratory bird groups had begun to return.

Even the coyotes investigated some of the other empty burrows to see whether they could enlarge the rooms and passageways. But then, they remembered why they were there, attempting to enter these empty burrows. The chipmunks were gone, and it seemed, they would never be back. Perhaps the coyotes missed being able to chase and stalk them. The coyotes noticed, alarmingly, that the trees were going too. The coyotes decided it was time to go back to scavenging in the liberal city of Olympia, where humans by the hundreds also scavenged and begged for their food. The coyotes left.

The few chipmunks left were a sorry lot, though they still sought the company of their own kind in a morning meet to try and plan for the next winter. The topic of discussion now was whether they should stay or go elsewhere. The trees were dead or dying. Of the pitifully little plant life left, the coastal ecosystems at the park were maintaining their tenacious hold. The shrunken forest line along the beach still had a few pine and oak.

The boy and his father who had arrived on a small motorized boat on the reach came back again in the summer, but as travelers to Tolmie State Park tended to, they stayed on the water and close to the beach. The boy sat on the deck one summer evening, straining his eyes beyond the first line of trees. Something told him that his visitor from the summer before was no longer there. The place was too still to relate to the many other small animals he had been able to view. The skies above, though, were filled with chattering blue jays, who seemed to be arguing about who was the most talented among them, who was the prettiest, and whose song rang the greatest.

The boy looked again. He was sure it was the skies he could glimpse beyond that first line of forest trees. The skies! What could have happened to the rest of the living vegetation? Something told him there was a great stillness afoot, apart from the blue jays—that the ecological system, for some reason, perhaps put out by these argumentative blue jays, had stilled itself. The various living and life systems were no longer supporting each other, feeding each other as they had done to maintain the great cycles of life, maintenance, and death.

It might now be only death that the boy was looking at. He hoped he wasn't right, but he couldn't be sure.

In truth, a small line of shrunken forest trees still hugged the beach, encircled by dense shrub swamps and evergreen shrubs. Further inland, brackish marshes had taken up position not too far from the reach. There were ponds too, at first vegetated by some sort of plant community from elsewhere in the park. Mother Nature had blessed the lily pond with the white flowers of water lilies, which covered its waters that first summer of the defeated chipmunks.

But without their normal propagation permitted by the smaller animals, carnivorous plants began to thrive in the boggy soil around the edge of other bogs and ponds. The carnivorous pitcher plants, bladderworts, sundews and butterworts, and the spectacular Venus flytrap snacked on unsuspecting insects.

These carnivorous plants grabbed whatever came their way, and Javlin, during one lazy eight survey, actually saw the flytrap close up on a clam. He came back again the next day, and the next, and decided that the clam had provided sustenance for three whole days, while the trap had remained closed. This time, he made sure that he only announced his discovery to his blue jays. He didn't want to lose any of his own sort to what had turned out to be one type of life making sure that another kind wouldn't survive.

Javlin was also very aware, as the ecosystems around him declined, that it was himself, and his tribe—who had earlier called themselves "hard-done-by" by those who had earned their sustenance—to have begun this war. He wondered idly whether this war would ever end, and when? The very next instant, he shook off the feeling. He had other business to attend to—his self-defense.

First, if the systems were collapsing, he would have to distance the blue jays from the blame.

The ecosystem at Tolmie State Park, like ecosystems everywhere, was a community of all that was living, along with the nonliving components of their environment (things like air, water, and mineral soil), interacting as a system. These biotic and abiotic components were regarded as linked together through nutrient cycles and energy flows. In truth, The Great War that had extinguished the life force of the chipmunks had interrupted a number of dynamic comings and goings within the park—the interactions between all the other living beings and their environment, blue jays included. And that was just in Tolmie State Park.

Old Owl and Hummingbird now said that the entire planet was an ecosystem. Not to be outdone, Javlin sent the oldest among them to find out how they could now save themselves. But it so happened that the blue jays now were facing some dissension among themselves. For the eldest had grown weary of the one who seemed to shoot his mouth off at every chance—Javlin. But they were also wary of the young upstarts among them—the mandolin playing, everything-for-all teen blue jays, who were known to occupy everything, not to mention ideas.

So the eldest lot poked about among the ecosystems here and out in the world, which Old Owl seemed to know about. They expounded that the energy that flows through ecosystems is obtained primarily from the sun. Voila! The sun could be blamed.

What it all boiled down to, in the end, was that they fed their mish-mash of information adjusted-to-fit, to Javlin. Javlin got up with his now rusty, squeaking, crumbling megaphone to announce that biodiversity had, maybe unwittingly, but no doubt unfavorably, affected ecosystem function, as had the processes of disturbance and succession, which had, in the normal course of matters, established themselves, the blue jays, and himself.

The sun had made an attempt after the snowbound cold of last winter. Their land had dried up, thanks to the sun's excessive focus of rays. What little vegetation was left was disappearing. Now, Javlin went on to say, "Global warming has been on the rise in the Earth's atmosphere and oceans for a little over a year now, and it will continue to be. Warming of the climate system is unequivocal, and it isn't just us. It is the increasing greenhouse gases produced by human activities such as the burning of fossil fuels and deforestation."

As was his habit, Javlin went straight for the kill. He pointed to humans and their motorized boats, holding up as an example the one with the boy and his father, who visited every summer, and even a couple of times before winter. They burnt fossil fuels to get here, he said. They didn't care about getting to the paradise that was Tolmie

State Park as fast as they could, never mind other hopefuls who had utilized their own wing power over pollution-ridden, globally-warmed habitats to reach Tolmie State Park. He was talking about his own kind, kindly.

Javlin also said that the chipmunks' demise had somehow upset the ecosystem, and even in death, the chipmunks were to blame. The trees were still dying as a result, and this far north land was warming up. Food was obviously short and more would die, but it was all the fault of the excessively powerful sun and global warming. Since Javlin was expounding, he warned of an even worse autumn and winter, this coming season. He warned of more extreme weather events.

The picture he drew of Tolmie State Park a year or more in the future, was, indeed, harsh. It was the fault of all those who had worked hard for hard times and had denuded their natural resources, he said. Javlin was still bad-mouthing the essentially do-good chipmunks, who had, in a way, held the ecosystem of Tolmie State Park together since its inception.

CHAPTER 7 – THE NEW BEGINNING

Two difficult winters had come and gone since the Great War that had signaled the end for Mitch and Tamias and most of their kind. Few chipmunks were left to search and gather, though they had endless larders now at their disposal in the underground burrows. Another middle-aged chipmunk now lived who greatly resembled the long-gone Mitch. His name, he said, was Animalia. And he said that he was descended from Mitch. The few remaining chipmunks still met early in the morning.

They discussed their seasonal plans and implementation for the day. The fewer blue jays were everywhere, but they paid the chipmunks no attention now. The chipmunks were too small a force, and no threat to their grasping ways. The tragedy was, there were also fewer blue jays wanting to grab and grasp all food stocks now, but there were very few foods to grasp.

With most of the forest cover nearly gone, the birds had fewer homes, unlike those on and under the ground. Fewer nests meant fewer offspring. In fact, the number of blue jays had come down to some two-thirds of their original number. Their leader, Javlin, had long since departed his mortal life, continuing to profess his line of philosophy about why the park had ceased to maintain and propagate its cyclical ecosystem.

The current, albeit depleted, generation of blue jays still held on to the chipmunk's greedy and biased ways, and, of course, global warming as being the main reason for all the malaise that had befallen Tolmie State Park. They also held on to the notion that the evil and now dead chipmunks, in conjunction with their human friends, had somehow inflicted this destruction. If there was an Animalia among the chipmunks, there now was a cocky little blue jay born off Javlin's offspring's nest on a grassy bush near the ground. His name was Jayvyn.

The hummingbirds had been coming back, immigrating in flocks over the spring and summer every year. But with a less paradisiacal park, their numbers had also dwindled. Gone were the colorful flowers that drew them in; gone was the delicious aroma of honeysuckle that once had covered large swathes of fertile ground.

News of the Tolmie State Park of old had spread far and wide among the hummingbirds of this part of the world and was the reason why flocks continued to immigrate there year after year. Hummingbird mothers still told their just-hatched babies nest stories about the park's aroma of cedar and pine, recognizable from miles away that had drawn them in. They still sang lullabies about the multitudes of orange-pink hyssop and red spring columbine, the horizontal seedpods of the cleome to swing on and nectar of scarlet cosmos, not to mention foxglove and goldenrod that used to be all over Tolmie State Park.

After the fourth year of returning in fewer and fewer numbers, hoping that some of the shrubs and plants would grow back, enough to support a profusion of even half the flowers that used to be, finally, the hummingbirds gave up. Their leader spoke of habitat loss and destruction as the sad, small flock flew away south for the last time, saying they wouldn't be back the next year.

It wasn't only the hummingbirds. Tolmie State Park's life hum was dying down.

The departing hummingbirds were to herald a mass exit, some by choice and some perforce. Everything that could fly or walk or crawl or tunnel through did what came naturally and followed the hummingbirds out of Tolmie State Park. The blue jays didn't like what they saw—they couldn't see much in the way of the blue jay diet of old, such as bark of oak and beech (the mighty oaks and beech trees had given up on life); nor was there anything by way of snails or caterpillars, grasshoppers or beetles, wild grapes or any of the berries that had been celebrated years ago during Wild Berry Week. Some of the blue jays argued for months about wanting to leave.

By the end of the fourth year, the trees of Tolmie State Park were all down and rotting. Even the owls hadn't remained. If their home, the great hollow in the aspen tree, had been created by a lightning bolt eons ago, heart rot had set in and caused the tree's demise. The owls simply winged slowly away in the direction of the towns and cities one autumn night. They left a message to say that they had had enough.

The birds were effectively gone, then, though the blue jays were still around still pleading their forefathers' innocence and letting loose a barrage of complaints against the chipmunks, who, they said, had wrought this devastation. And what of the land mammals? Tolmie State Park had given up its packs of coyotes long ago. The coyotes had found a life closer to luxury, they said. They lived among the bushes and bins on the great city's outskirts, and they were happy with scraps of meat, which came cooked, in the manner that city people liked them. Foraging in bins was better than chasing live targets, which could also skitter and sadly die, as the chipmunks had, said the coyotes, young and old. The blue jays rejoiced every time another group of animals departed the park. The blue jays coined the mass exodus as "Fur Flight."

The bears, with their winter hibernation, would have loved the city life, provided they could cuddle into a cottage with a bed and a blanket, but since they preferred the wilds further north, that was the direction in which they traveled. The pitifully few chipmunks, skunks, and weasels left with their noses held up high, with Animalia talking and advising them all the way, collecting foods and storing them in their chipmunk cheek stores.

Was anybody or anything left?

Yes. The rodents and skitters said it was too late for them to find any other place to live. So it was with the insects—the crickets were minus their trees and shrubs, but the ants were still happy to run around, carry the smallest nutritive load home to their burrows and tunnels, and to wait it out for the winter, occasionally bumping into a snake in another tunnel or burrow.

Baby ants demanded to know in their underground cradles at bedtime what happened to Tolmie State Park of yesteryear. The matron ant would tell and retail the story how the chipmunks were known to be busy a great part of the year, especially from autumn till the winter, with harvesting and hoarding tree seeds and putting away stores of food for themselves. The stored seeds, however, played a crucial role in seeding other plants, some of which grew, over many, many years, into trees.

The matron ant also explained without the chipmunks, the seeding had simply ceased and the trees perished because the ecosystem had been halted in its cyclical continuity. She said that without the chipmunks to do all the hard work, the "economy" of the ecosystem had simply failed. The other land animals of the park, the beaver and the deer, the coyote and the reptiles, which normally contributed to the ecosystem, might have actually helped destroy the ecosystem by not contributing, since they all left the part as well.

The matron ant would always finish with, "The blue jays brought a cancer with them to the park and that cancer grew and grew until nearly all life was gone. Before the cancer grew, there was a time when the waters out in the reach rippled with the passing of the currents and the swaying marine plants seen close to the surface. The beach was sandy, as most beaches are, but the first row of wind breakers were the first row of woodland trees."

The baby ants would interrupt the matron ant now, with a "But what are woodland trees?" And she would have to describe a most wondrous natural growth that even she could never fully imagine.

"Trees still exist in all other state parks. I'm going to start at the top, at the crown, which consists of the leaves and branches. Our queen ant wears a crown, but it isn't as magnificent as the crown of a tree. It is made up of living green leaves, which help cool the air by providing shade and reduce the impact of raindrops on the soil below. The leaves are the food factories of a tree. The tree food is either used or stored in the branches, trunk, and roots. Trees make oxygen, which all of us need to breathe, to live.

The trunk, branches, and twigs of the tree are covered with bark. If you go to sleep now, I will take you on an outing to look for scraps of long discarded bark tomorrow."

And so the insects would dream of plants and of trees and hope that someday, Tolmie State Park might be able to sprout one. They also hoped that someday they would see their friends, the chipmunks—that the little workers would somehow come back and help them raise the wonderland that was Tolmie State Park again.

Was it possible?

It was, but not in the manner of the instant return-to-paradise pictured by the ants. They would have to live with the now-freezing, at times warm, vast flat land devoid of anything but their scurrying selves for a long, long time. Far in the distance, they could see the sunlight rippling on the waters of Puget Sound. Still further, were the high snow-covered Olympic Mountains.

The ants hoped, they planned, and they thought they could see to the implementation of those plans. They might just be able to set the park right. They might just be able to get the cycle going again.

Tolmie State Park could get back to the way it used to be many, many years ago when the chipmunks scurried about, setting up the first link in the ecological cycle, when their burrows drew the oxygen of these trees right into the soil, long before the strange blue jays had arrived, with their notions of taking from others what they thought should be theirs. The ants had much work to do.

The ants dug their still more miniature tunnels. They scurried about, carrying, and sometimes passing on to each other, the tiniest of seeds. They carried these for their own storehouses, but they didn't know that it would benefit still more seeding, when one tiny seed began to germinate in its underground store. The seed drew energy from the outside, from the sun's rays, unmindful of global warming, and its shoot shot right through layers of soil.

The ants had, unwittingly, begun the process of a new tree life.

Word got around through the birds in the air, the insects underground. The first four-legged creatures came to investigate at the park's edge. So did a group of tortoises, half-swimming and half-walking ponderously in from the beach. They swung their short necks from side-to-side under their shells and took it all in—the brand new Tolmie State Park. They spoke slowly, but they knew Tolmie Animal-Language. Their great-great-great-great-grandparents had simply passed it down.

And they carried their slow speech elsewhere. There were others who understood—the weasels and sea lions, the bats of the night and their partners, the owls. Far away, in another state park further east, other four-legged animals heard, the squirrels and chipmunks with stripes down their backs among them. Some of them had been passed on the story of the great Tolmie State Park and the great spirit of a chipmunk known as Mitch.

A small group of chipmunks led by Chip, a descendant of Animalia and Mitch, arrived at Tolmie State Park so they can undertake their chipmunk tasks. Now, it was up to Chip, progeny of the far-sighted Animalia, as his mother had informed him when he was but little, to decide that he would like to see the place from which his ancestors had come.

And so it happened that one morning, when the sun rose sharp at seven-thirty, casting its rays over the new leaves of the relatively new trees of Tolmie State Park, that the ants, the beetles, the tortoises, and the bats (who were arranging to fold up for the big sleep of the day) and the owls (who wished for a hollow, but had none, in the brand new trees), saw a sea of returning chipmunks, with Chip at their head.

The sea of chipmunks was squeaking and chattering in Tolmie State Park's Animal Language. Their speech indicated that they had returned to the Promised Land.

They spread all over the park, looking for comfort spots and places where they could dig their homes. For the old burrows had all been filled in years ago, when the earth, unsupported by tree roots, had simply caved in on them. But the new trees were spreading new roots now. And the caved in burrows, had, in a way, turned the underground soil, so that it was fresh soil to which the new roots were reaching out.

The leader of the chipmunks, Chip, found a strong, brand new root that had grown in an arch above ground. He dug at the ground within the root arch with his small paws, though in this task he was joined by his wife of the last few months, and a friend chipmunk, who had elected to be their neighbor if they decided to stay on in Tolmie State Park.

They dug a good entrance to a burrow that day. The space would help shelter them for their first night. The next day, Chip was up early, scurrying around, still discovering new foods and fruits, seeds and insects. He pinched himself so he could believe he had been successful in his mission. Now, he would have to handle the rest of the year, and advise his fellow chipmunks about how best to settle in Tolmie State Park.

They would have to have an early morning meet. There was much to do.

And so animals of all kinds came back to the new Tolmie State Park and got the cycle going. That autumn, the owls saw a chipmunk hauling a long pink worm to the second row of yew, where most of the chipmunks had their burrows. The burrows were filling up fast with winter stores, for when the small creatures would go into semi-hibernation, they would fill their stomachs with all the nutrition they had taken such pains to store over months.

They wouldn't have to emerge out on the frost and snow, which blanketed the trees, the ground, and even the lakes and the shoreline in January. The chipmunks would be snug. The trees, in turn, would strip down to their bare minimums, which would conserve their energy so their leaves and buds would be able to emerge when spring came.

That was when the chipmunk babies would emerge and the birds' eggs hatch. That would be when the land would burst forth once more before the creatures, who must conserve, set about doing their job. How else would the natural environment thrive?

It had taken a great deal of time and many years, but the hard working animals and insects had eventually proven themselves right, as Mitch had hoped, long ago. They worked and saved not only for their own existence, but for the cycles of nature, for all. As for those who had wrecked what one group had made possible, the animals and trees of Tolmie State Park had promised to stand together to make sure they wouldn't revisit the park now or ever in the future.

Thank You!

Thank you for reading *The Haves and Have Nots.* I hope you enjoyed reading it as much as I enjoyed writing it. If you enjoyed this book, I would deeply appreciate it if you took a few minutes and write a short review on Amazon.com. Reviews are absolutely vital to a book's success and authors such as myself enjoy reading about want readers have to say.

One more thing! I wrote *The Haves and Have Nots* because liberal values are replacing conservative values, thus destroying America's greatness. If the corrupt nature of liberalism is exposed, maybe, America's greatness may return. So please help spread the word about this conservative-focused book. Yes, of course, I could use the extra exposure, but so do our conservative believes!

Arthur M. Mills, Jr.

ABOUT THE AUTHOR

Arthur M. Mills, Jr.'s third grade teacher read Roald Dahl's *Charlie and the Chocolate Factory* to the class and then asked the students to write a one-page sequel to the book. Arthur couldn't stop writing, and it was then that Arthur knew he would be a writer.

Arthur M. Mills, Jr. is a full-time husband, father, and Warrant Officer in the U.S. Army. If that isn't busy enough, he's also a full-time author. Arthur is the creator of *Branching Plot Books*, a book series devoted to the art of double meanings and reader interaction. *Branching Plot Books* include the award-winning part-memoir and part-fiction novel *The Empty Lot Next Door* and the teen/young adult interactive fiction novel *The Crawl Space*, as well as the modern day fable *The Haves and Have Nots*. Arthur and his wife, Yonsun, have two children, Arthur and Allen.

For more information about Arthur and his writing, please visit the following:

Websites

www.branchingplotbooks.com

www.thehavesandhavenots.com

www.the-crawl-space.com

www.theemptylotnextdoor.com

Social Media

https://www.facebook.com/RantingManifesto

https://www.facebook.com/TheEmptyLotNextDoor

https://www.facebook.com/thecrawlspace.interactive

The Empty Lot Next Door

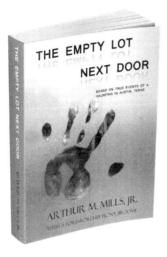

Whether or not you believe in ghosts, the true life experience of Arthur M. Mills, Jr. deserves consideration. Find out who Candle Face was, her taunting behavior, and how she turned a boy's childhood into a living nightmare in *The Empty Lot Next Door*.

Ray (Arthur's childhood name) and his family have just moved into a small house beside a strange, vacant lot where another house once stood, and where a huge wide hole mysteriously awaits the brave or foolhardy. Ray and his friends consider the empty lot just an exciting playground until Ray hears tales of how the lot's house burned down years ago, leaving a girl to die in the fire. According to the neighborhood kids, the little girl will come out at night to haunt anyone who dares to jump into the empty lot's hole.

Both frightened and intrigued, Ray decides to test the validity of the tale. When he jumps into the hole to challenge the ghost, nothing happens. But in the night, Ray sees a figure emerge from the hole who makes eye contact with him. Soon, Ray is haunted by Candle

Face. She visits his dreams and leaves handprints and other terrifying signs for him even when he is awake.

The Crawl Space

The Crawl Space by Arthur M. Mills, Jr. is an interactive teen / young adult novel about bullying, punishment, and redemption that allows the reader to make choices for the three main characters and to realize every decision in life is not ultimately black and white, or right or wrong.

Bruce, Mark, and Charles have long been the school bullies, tormenting younger and weaker kids. But they go too far the day they try to make a student enter the dreaded crawl space under the school stage. Everyone knows the crawl space is haunted by a boy who entered it and never came out. When the school principal catches the boys, she punishes them by having them clean out the crawl space by themselves over the weekend. Alone in the school at night, the three boys soon discover that the crawl space is not the only part of the school that is haunted. Together, the boys must make difficult choices if they are to survive, and they need the reader to help them make those decisions.

Made in the USA
San Bernardino, CA
24 June 2014